MW00803359

Cheering
For the
Home Team

DAN QUELLO

HARVEST HOUSE PUBLISHERS
Eugene, Oregon 97402

Illustrations by Lynda Adkins

CHEERING FOR THE HOME TEAM

Copyright © 1992 by Harvest House Publishers
Eugene, Oregon 97402

Library of Congress Cataloging-in-Publication Data

Quello, Dan, 1941-
    Cheering for the home team / Dan Quello.
    Summary: Discusses the relationship between brothers and sisters
and how cooperation can create a smoother, more pleasant family life.
    ISBN 0-89081-917-3
    1. Sibling rivalry—Juvenile literature.   2. Brothers and sisters--
Juvenile literature   3. Competition (Psychology)—Juvenile literature.   4. Family—Juvenile literature.   [1. Brothers and sisters.   2. Sibling rivalry.]   I. Title.
BF723.S43Q45   1992
646.7'8—dc20   92-3099
                                                                  CIP
                                                                  AC

Printed in the United States of America.

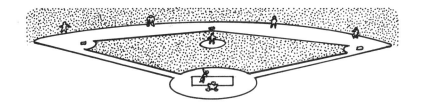

Contents

1. You Gotta Help Me! 5

2. A Solid Hit 9

3. An Angry Kick 15

4. Baseball Heaven 19

5. Hero Time 23

6. Out of the Park 27

   Judd Powers' Notebook 33
   THE HOME TEAM

You Gotta Help Me!

*B*aseball heaven"...that's how best friends Scooter and Jess talked about their chance to attend Judd Powers' All-Star camp. A week away from home. Competing with some of the best athletes in the state. It was the stuff dreams were made of.

And to learn the game from Judd Powers! Even moms who didn't like baseball liked Judd Powers—mostly because he was so good-looking.

Judd had made a name for himself playing 12 years in the majors. Offering this six-day camp to promising young players was

Judd's way of giving something back to the game he loved.

Tryouts for the team from Watkins County would be Saturday morning at Civic Stadium. Scooter knew—he had the date circled on his calendar.

What he just found out was that Kevin had marked the date on his calendar too.

Kevin was Scooter's kid brother. Even though he was a year-and-a-half younger than Scooter, he had long legs and was almost as tall. Since turning 12 two weeks ago, Kevin was now eligible to try out for the same select team.

Slipping into his father's den, where he went to make his most important calls, Scooter pushed the buttons that put him in touch with Jess.

"You gotta help me," Scooter whispered into the phone. "Kevin is gonna try out for our team! If he makes it, our time is ruined. Can you imagine your kid brother tagging along for a week? You gotta help me, Jess. We've gotta come up with a plan!"

Over a tray of toasted cheese sandwiches in the school cafeteria, a plan was hatched.

"Make him look bad," said Jess, looking around to make sure no one else could hear.

"If he blows tryouts, he stays home. It's as simple as that."

"I like it!" said Scooter. "We can talk to some of the guys. Drop his throws. Throw wide to him. Don't give him anything good to swing at. With a little help, he'll look bad."

"Totally bad!" laughed Jess.

"Not too obvious, though," cautioned Scooter. "If my mom or dad find out, I'm history!"

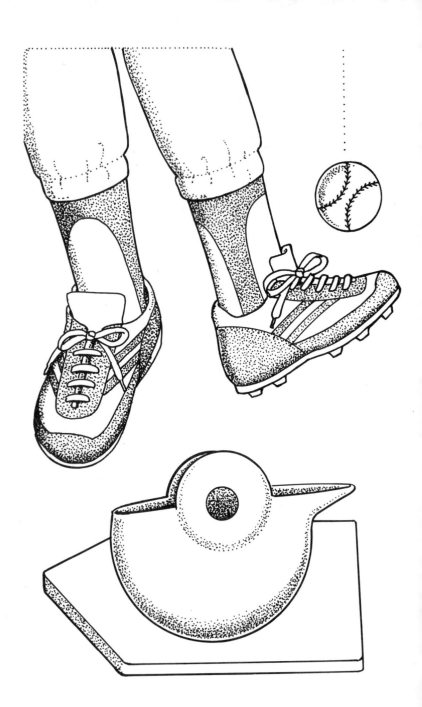

2

A
Solid Hit

*A*s the young hopefuls began arriving at Civic Stadium, the talk centered on who would most likely make the team. By most accounts young Kevin was given a good shot. Like his older brother, he was a good athlete.

Mr. Sullivan, the junior high coach, had been put in charge of tryouts. After some hitting and fielding, he announced a full game scrimmage. Hoots and hollers filled the air. High-fives clapped overhead.

"No better conditions than gamelike to see what a fella can do," muttered Coach Sullivan as he began tapping players on the head, pushing them off to one of two scrimmage teams.

Two batters into the first inning, Scooter's friend B.J., playing at shortstop, scooped up a grounder and fired it at close range to Kevin, playing at second. The ball came so fast that Kevin could only duck as the ball shot past him into right field.

"Come on, chicken!" B.J. hollered. "Let's at least stop 'em. We could've had a double play!"

Two batters later, crack!... another sharp grounder. This one came up the middle to Kevin. He fielded it, then bobbled it slightly, but recovered in time to make the throw to first. With a bit of a stretch he thought Scooter could have caught it. But he seemed to let it glance off his glove, into the dugout behind him. A sure out was turned into a double.

"Nice going, Kev!" B.J. moaned, loud enough for Coach Sullivan to hear. Then, becoming softer, but still loud enough for the infielders to overhear, he teased, "If it weren't for gravity... Kev couldn't hit the ground!"

Coach Sullivan heard it and barked, "That's enough!"

Batting didn't go much better for Kevin. With Jess on the mound, everything was coming in either low or outside. Not having done well at fielding, Kevin knew it was important for him to do well at batting.

At his first trip to the plate he took four balls for a walk. This time he would have to do better. With a count of three balls and two strikes, Kevin decided, even before Jess began his windup, that he would swing at his next pitch.

Whiff! "Strike three!" called the ump.

It was the top of the seventh inning before Kevin got his next turn at bat. This would be it! He felt it in his bones. If Jess was going to keep throwing low and wide, Kevin would just have to crowd the plate.

Grinning widely, Jess wound up and whipped one high and inside. Kevin sprang back, catching his balance with his bat.

Taking a moment to readjust his helmet, he backed out of the batter's box. Before stepping back in, he tapped the end of the bat against his shoes. First the left foot . . . then the right. Once more, Kevin stepped forward and hugged the plate.

Jess stretched, took a slower-than-usual windup, and delivered. Nobody was prepared for what happened next.

Kevin recoiled . . . but not quick enough. The ball found its mark—a direct hit to the left side of Kevin's face. The force of the ball popped his helmet off and into the air.

Scooter's heart leaped as he saw his brother spin and fall to the ground.

An Angry Kick

C oach Sullivan threw down his notepad and rushed to the batter's box. Dropping to his knees, he cupped Kevin's head in his hands. "Get me some ice!" he hollered as he motioned with his head for the players to move back.

Blood and saliva trickled out the sides of Kevin's mouth. It mingled with the dust and tears already on his face.

Scooter glanced over his shoulder to Jess. Their eyes connected. For a long moment he let them bore into Jess. It was a look that didn't need words.

Stepping backward slowly, away from the

other players, Jess stammered, "I didn't mean to do it . . . I was just trying to brush him . . . push him back . . . you know, so he wouldn't get a hit. Remember? *our* plan."

"Yeah, I remember," said Scooter, fighting back the tears. "I said make him look bad . . . not kill him!"

The trip to the emergency room confirmed what everyone knew: Kevin's jaw was busted . . . but good! The doctor said the X-ray showed it to be fractured in three places. After resetting it, a stainless steel brace was fitted around Kevin's head. It hurt Kevin even to talk. But then, he didn't have much to say.

Taking the long way home from Civic Stadium, Scooter and Jess took turns kicking a smooth, gray stone. As it came Jess' turn, he gave it an angry kick and said, "I was only trying to help."

"Some help!" Scooter mumbled. "I can't believe this. All I wanted was for Kevin not to come to camp. Now he's got a busted face and I feel rotten."

The rest of the way home these two friends were mostly silent. As they neared the driveway to his house Jess asked haltingly, "Should we just tell him? I mean, tell him . . . and say we're sorry?"

"No way!" snarled Scooter.

As promised, Coach Sullivan posted the names of those chosen to attend Judd Powers' All-Star Camp. On a bulletin board, just outside the main entrance to Civic Stadium, there was Scooter's name. About halfway down on the right side, there was Jess' name too.

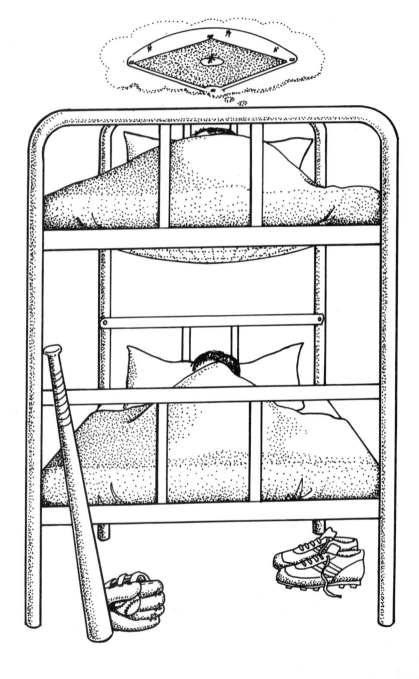

4

Baseball Heaven

*J*udd Powers' Baseball Camp was everything it had been cracked up to be. Except for the cooked carrots, it *was* heaven!

And Judd Powers. He wasn't as big as Scooter thought he might be, but he was impressive. His family was something special too. You could see the love Judd felt for his wife . . . the way they held hands as they walked around the camp.

Their daughter Jodee was one of the most fun girls Scooter or Jess had ever met. The fact is, almost every boy in camp had a crush on her. Too bad, though, because Jodee was more interested in playing ball than she was in boys!

Still, Jess and Scooter felt pretty lucky when Judd asked the team from Watkins County if they would mind having Jodee spend the week working out with their team. Mind? They loved it!

As the players got to know Judd and his family, they often kidded and teased like one big family. Some of the campers liked to mimic Judd . . . the way he pushed his cap up on his forehead and said, "Baseball, ya know . . . everything you need to know about life . . . it's in this game!"

Each night, following the evening meal, the campers gathered in the fireside room to hear Judd, or one of the assistants, talk about some aspect of the game of baseball.

Wednesday night's topic seemed almost out of place. Judd was the speaker, and his topic was "The Home Team: Getting Along with Your Brothers and Sisters at Home."

Judd had barely gotten the words out of his mouth when Scooter's mind raced back to Kevin, sidelined at home. The whole scene of Kevin being hit and lying in the batter's box flashed across his mind. The same awful feelings returned to his gut.

"The families that get along best," Judd began his talk that night, *"are those who think of themselves as a TEAM."*

And then, in more ways than anyone at camp could have imagined, Judd passed out a fistfull of notes showing how key ideas from the game of baseball could make them better team-players at home.

Maybe because of all that had happened, Scooter was more open to hearing what Judd had to say that night. But as he talked on, Scooter had this strange feeling that Judd was talking straight to his heart.

Scooter didn't dare say anything out loud, but inside he wondered: Is this how God talks to people today? He understood that in Bible times God spoke to people through prophets. But with not too many of those around anymore, maybe God had to use baseball players like Judd. Scooter didn't know, but he wondered.

As he climbed into his top bunk that night, he had a lot to think about. He had *another* team to which he belonged . . . a Home Team!

5

Hero Time

Nobody could believe that tomorrow was the last day of camp. The event toward which the week was moving was the All-Camp World Series. Each of the six teams would be facing off for the camp championship.

The idea of the tournament being held on the final day of camp was to give moms and dads coming to pick up their kids a chance to see how the players had improved.

The morning games were over and the championship game was well underway when Scooter spotted his dad, Kevin, and sister Kelly finding their place in the stands behind third base. Scooter glanced their way a couple of times between innings as he came to the dugout, tossing his glove atop the roof. Otherwise, while batting or playing first base, he practically forgot that they were there.

It was not the kind of game that most people enjoy watching, even loyal parents. It was what Judd called "a defensive battle."

Scooter and Jess' team, wearing gray uniforms with thin dark blue stripes, had only two hits and no runs going into the seventh inning. The opposing team, wearing off-white uniforms with red stripes, had knocked out four hits, but only scored one run.

The eighth inning and top of the ninth produced little in the way of fireworks from the batter's box. Both pitchers retired their sides without so much as a foul ball being hit.

With one out in the bottom of the ninth, the gray team sent Judd's daughter Jodee to the plate. Some thought it a bit risky to put her in at such a crucial time, but Jodee was cool under pressure. She hit the first pitch thrown to her for a line-drive single. With Jodee safely on first, the team wondered why they hadn't use her earlier.

B.J. was next up to bat. Grinning widely, he sensed his opportunity to be the game's hero. A round tripper here would give them not only the lead, but the championship.

He watched the first two go by. Both of them were strikes, but higher than he liked 'em. Waving the tip of his bat in a small circular motion, B.J. waited eagerly for just the right pitch.

The sharp sound of the bat smacking the ball sent the left-fielder back to the fence. Going a few steps to his left, he reached out, pulled it in, and with one smooth motion whipped the ball to the shortstop. B.J. was out. But Jodee had advanced safely to second.

Two out, runner at second, bottom of the ninth, and down one run.

6

Out of the Park

S cooter took a deep breath as he walked slowly from the on-deck circle to the plate. His heart was pounding.

"Come on, Scooter!" came the chant from the dugout. "Hit away, Scooter!" "You can do it!"

"Strike one!" called the ump as Scooter stood still as a statue.

Not wanting to strike out without so much as taking a cut at the ball, Scooter determined to go for the next pitch if it was anywhere near the strike zone.

Whiff! "Strike Two!" cried the ump.

Scooter had dreamed of situations like

this, when winning it all would come down to him. Now that such a moment had come, he wondered, what was so great about it?

As Scooter awaited the next pitch, it seemed as though everything was now in slow motion. The windup . . . the pitch . . . the ball coming down the pike.

Scooter's shoulders rotated forward. His bat uncocked, a mere extension of his arms. If ever bat were to meet ball, this was it.

It was beautiful. The ball floating out of the park. The fans coming to their feet.

That split second of fantasy turned into an eternity of sheer terror. His bat hit nothing but air. The ump's call, "Strike three!" broke his trance.

Scooter's mouth dropped . . . but nothing came out. All that was heard was a collective sigh of disappointment from the Watkins County side of the field.

Scooter stood alone. His head dropped to his chest. Players from across the field rushed to the mound to hoist the winning pitcher atop their shoulders.

From behind him, Scooter felt an arm come up around his shoulder. A voice that was familiar, yet slurred, said: "It's okay. Nobody could get a hit off him today. It's okay."

A tear welled in Scooter's eye as he turned to see the afternoon sun bounce off a stainless steel brace that told him it was Kevin.

Getting a hold of himself, Scooter turned to look his brother in the eye. "No, it's not okay. I mean, striking out and letting my team down . . . that'll be okay. But letting you down . . . what I did to you . . . that was not okay.

"I don't know what you know about it . . . Jess hitting you at tryouts. But it was really *my* fault. We tried to make you look bad so you wouldn't come to camp.

"I never intended it to go as far as it did. What I did was wrong, Kevin, but it won't be wasted.

"I've learned some things up here . . . about baseball, for sure, but more than that, about myself . . . things that will make me a better brother."

Walking over to where Dad and Kelly stood waiting, Scooter threw his arm around Kevin. "What I learned up here," he went on, "probably more than anything else, is that what makes for a good ball team makes for a good home team as well!"

Coming to a stop at the side of Dad's car, Scooter pulled Kelly into his side and said,

"Just you wait . . . your ol' brother is going to show you!"

Then, turning toward Kevin, he looked for a long moment into his eyes, still a bit puffed up from where he had been hit by the ball. "We probably won't be playing on the same ball team this year," said Scooter, "but maybe we can still be teammates."

As Dad started up the car, a warm smile broke across Kevin's face. "I think I could like this—what do you call it?—cheering for the Home Team!"

Judd Powers' Notebook

The Home Team

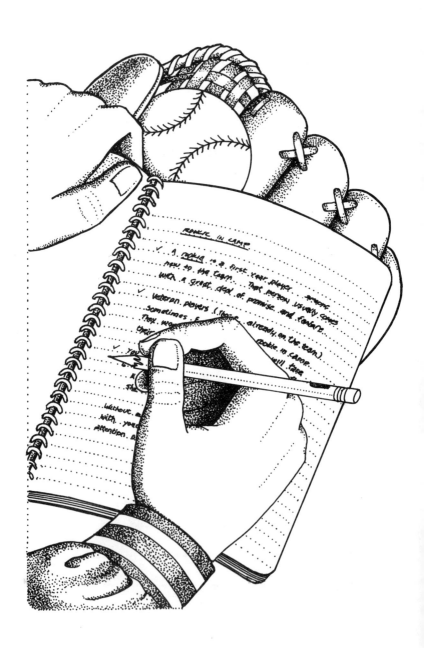

The families that get along best think of themselves as a TEAM!

Being born or adopted into a family is much like being welcomed onto a team. From the start, you are the center of much attention and love.

As you grow and learn new skills, you will want to use them for the good of the family. It is your way of making a place for yourself. . . a place to belong . . .

. . . on the Home Team!

1 Rookie in Camp

A rookie is a first-year player...someone *new* to the team. That person usually comes with a great deal of promise and fanfare. Veteran players (those already on the team) sometimes feel uneasy with a rookie in camp. They worry that the new player will take their place or cut down on their playing time.

You may have feelings like that when a new brother or sister is welcomed into the family.

> Example. "Baby sister is cute all right, but will she take too much of Mom and Dad's time?"

Without even knowing it, you begin competing with your brother or sister for the love and attention of Mom and Dad.

2 The Lineup

In baseball, the *lineup* is the order in which each player comes to bat. The lineup is prepared by the manager, and once the game begins, it cannot be changed.

The order in which you were born into your family might be called the family lineup.

- If you are the youngest, there may be times when you think it would be neat to be the oldest.
- Older children sometimes envy the youngest.
- Middle children may wish to change places with either the older or younger child.

As in baseball, once the lineup is set, it cannot be changed. Fortunately, *there are advantages and disadvantages to each postion.*

3 Competition

Competition is an important part of the game of baseball. Besides competing against other teams, players of the same team often compete with one another. This kind of competition brings out the best in us. *As we compete with others, we discover what we can and cannot do well.*

Sometimes, without even knowing it, brothers and sisters compare themselves to each other. By discovering what you do well, you find your own place in the family.

> Example: If one child is good at music, another may find his or her interest in sports.

As each one finds his or her niche in the family, he finds not only a place to belong but also a way to contribute to the good of the team!

Contracts

There are a few rules to which both players and coaches must agree. To show that they understand the rules and agree to follow them, both players and coaches sign a *contract*.

Many people think it is a good idea for family members to agree on their own set of rules. You may choose to include such things as:

- No shouting in the house.
- Complete homework assignments before watching TV
- You may wear what belongs to a brother or sister only by permission.

Family living goes a lot better when everyone is *clear about the rules and has agreed to live by them.*

5 Team Meeting

For teams to work well together, they must spend time talking and listening to each other. At a *team meeting* players set aside one hour each week for the purpose of coming together and discussing matters that affect the whole team.

Many families have found that setting aside one hour each week gives them a chance to discuss matters that affect the whole family.

When you know what the concerns of your family are, and have a chance to pray about them together, you are on your way to working things out!

6 Calling for the Ball

When two fielders go after the same high fly ball, it is necessary for one of them to call out "I've got it!" The other player then backs away and avoids a collision on the field.

Sometimes brothers and sisters want the same thing at the same time. It could be a toy, game, or book. Unless one of you calls out "I've got it!" and the other backs off, you could end up fighting over it.

To be fair, you will need to take turns at being first. You might say to your sister, "You play with it for 20 minutes, and then it's my turn." *You will discover a good feeling inside you when you are unselfish toward others.*

7 A Glove not for Sharing

Most of the things used by ballplayers are the property of the whole team—the clubhouse, dugout, bases, bats, and balls, to name just a few. Yet each player also has some personal equipment . . . things not meant to be shared. A player's glove, for example, is a very personal thing.

Many of the things in your house are there for the whole family to enjoy. The TV, stereo, and encyclopedias are intended for everyone's use. Yet each of you also has some personal things . . . your own private property.

You may want to have an understanding with your brothers and sisters that all personal items . . . clothes, tapes, and bicycles . . . may be used only with permission.

8 Easy on the Ump!

The players who hit, catch, and throw the ball are not the only people on the field. There are two to four umpires out there as well. Their job is to judge everything that happens on the field, to keep the game as fair for everyone as possible.

Parents, stepparents, and grandparents are sometimes expected to act as umpires... always available to settle your quarrels and disputes.

Most of the time, however, *it is best if your parents do not have to interfere with your squabbles.* Setting up your own rules and maybe improving them as you go are important steps in learning how to get along with other people.

9

In a Slump

When a baseball player is in a slump, he is not performing well in a certain aspect of his game. Generally a good hitter, a player who goes five or six games without hitting the ball, is said to be "in a slump."

Occasionally you or a brother or sister may find yourself "in a slump."

- Generally a good student, you may experience a string of bad test scores.
- Usually on good terms with your little sister, now you're mostly fighting because she always wants to tag along.

The best way *out* of a slump is *through* it! Keep at it. In time things will work out.

Also, if a brother or sister is in a slump, you can help by not teasing. Rather, *look for ways to encourage one another.*

10 Embarrassing Errors

A badly thrown ball or a fielding mistake which allows another player to get on base undeservedly is called an *error*. Nobody likes to make an error, and yet at one time or another most of us do.

It can be embarrassing to make a mistake.

If we make too many of them, we get discouraged.

It is helpful to think of mistakes as learning opportunities. *From our errors we can learn a better way!*

The next time you goof up in your family, think of it as a present to yourself...a chance to learn a new and better way of getting along.

11 An Assist

A baseball team is more than nine individual players each trying to do his best. A good baseball team is nine players each *trying to make the OTHER player look good as well!*

- They back each other up on defense.
- They get on base so that the next batter can score a run.

It's one player helping another to look good!

When one player contributes to a put-out by making a good stop or a brilliant throw, he is credited with an *assist*. He didn't make the actual out, but he assisted the one who did.

Examples of assists for the Home Team:

- Help a younger sister with a math problem.
- Assist an older brother with his turn at washing dishes when he's in a hurry.

An assist is any unselfish act which helps another person to look good!

12 Infield Chatter

If you get close enough to the playing field, you will hear lots of chatter coming from the infield players. That steady flow of encouraging words is being spoken to the pitcher. Such phrases as "Atta boy," "Come on now," or "You got 'im" are all meant to help the pitcher do his best.

Words of encouragement are just as important to say at home as they are on the playing field.

When you say to a brother or sister—

- "Nice job!"
- "Way to go!" or
- "That looks hard, but I know you can do it!"—

you are instilling confidence in your brother or sister.

If you haven't spoken words like that to each other before, it may seem strange to you at first. But once you begin, you will find that this kind of chatter is just as valuable at home as it is on the playing field.

13 Relief Pitcher

While most pitchers would like to complete the games they begin, not all of them do. If they start to feel tired or sore, a relief pitcher is brought into the game. A *relief pitcher* is one who completes what someone else has started.

Occasionally a brother or sister may start a project and not be able to finish it. When you—

- Help an older brother finish his job of mowing the lawn
- Fold a basket of clothes which your sister has washed—

you are doing the work of a relief pitcher!

14 Learning to Lose

Enjoying victories and suffering defeats are all a part of baseball. When you test your skills against another person, you sometimes win and sometimes lose.

The competition that you feel between your brothers and sisters can be very natural. Whether in sports, music, or grades, it's one way of measuring how you're doing.

It is not okay, however, if you use these comparisons to conclude that you are a better or worse person than your brother or sister. You don't have to come out on top all the time to be a good person.

Winners are those who do their best. The only losers are those who never try!

Team Spirit

One difference between teams that do well and those that don't is an invisible thing called *team spirit*.

Team spirit means that the good of the whole team is more important than the *wishes of any one player*. This means that occasionally a player will have to sacrifice his own interests for the good of the team as a whole.

Examples of team spirit:

- Dad getting up early to help son deliver papers on a stormy morning.
- Sis giving up a trip to the beach so the whole family can make the trip to Grandma's.

Team spirit is contagious. *Terrific things can happen when family members work together and begin "cheering for the Home Team"!*

Other Youth Books from Harvest House

Katie's World Adventure Series
A new series for boys and girls

Curious, inquisitive Katie Thompsen loves adventure, loves to travel, and most of all loves to write everything in her diary. So when Katie's journalist father takes the family to faraway places, mystery and misadventure are sure to follow.

You will catch glimpses of the culture and customs of different countries and share Katie's reflections through glimpses into her secret diary. But Katie Thompsen is a special girl because she loves Jesus and loves to learn about living the Christian life.

You'll share it all as you discover this exciting new collection of books, the joy of *Katie's World*.

Katie's Swiss Adventure

Katie Sails the Nile

Katie's Russian Holiday

Katie Goes to New York

Katie and the Amazon Mystery

Katie—Lost in the South Seas

Books That Help the Hurts of Children

by Dan Quello

Each of the exciting new *Books That Help the Hurts of Children* focuses on a particular area of emotional pain or family conflict through an allegorical story written on a child's level for ages 8 through 13.

SAFELY THROUGH THE STORM

"This book can be enormously helpful to children who are afloat in the troubled waters of divorce. The brevity and charming illustrations make it easy reading while delivering a powerful message."

—Ann Landers

When the two people you love the most decide to break apart—life is very tough. That's how it is for *1.5 million* kids every year who become children of divorce.

In a sensitive book that recognizes the turbulent feelings children experience in the wake of divorce, author Dan Quello helps young readers understand their struggles over their parents' divorce. Comparing life to a voyage at sea, and divorce to a violent storm the family has encountered, Quello illustrates God's promise to stay beside us during the roughest times. This book offers the assurance that kids need to make it safely through the troubled waters of divorce.